EASY BOOKS

DETROIT PUBLIC LIBRARY

3 5674 02961762 1

TITLE W

P9-EMH-109

DETROIT PUBLIC LIBRARY
SHERWOOD FOREST LIBRARY
7117 W. Seven Mile Rd.
Detroit, MI 48221

DATE DUE

BC-3

JAN 2 0 2001

SF

Little Bunny
On the Move

To my wife and best friend,
Yunhee,
And our daughter,
Suki

Henry Holt and Company, LLC, *Publishers since 1866*
115 West 18th Street, New York, New York 10011

Henry Holt is a registered trademark of Henry Holt and Company, LLC

Copyright © 1999 by Peter McCarty
All rights reserved.
Published in Canada by Fitzhenry & Whiteside Ltd.,
195 Allstate Parkway, Markham, Ontario L3R 4T8.

Library of Congress Cataloging-in-Publication Data
McCarty, Peter. Little bunny on the move / by Peter McCarty.
Summary: A little bunny rabbit hurries past five fat sheep, over train
tracks, and across an open field on his way to a special destination.
[1. Rabbits—Fiction. 2. Home—Fiction.] I. Title.
PZ7.M47841327Li 1999 [E]—dc21 98-29787

ISBN 0-8050-4620-8 / First Edition—1999
Printed in the United States of America on acid-free paper. ∞
The artist used pencils and watercolor on 140-pound watercolor paper
to create the illustrations for this book.
3 5 7 9 10 8 6 4

Little Bunny On the Move

WRITTEN AND ILLUSTRATED BY

Peter McCarty

HENRY HOLT AND COMPANY
NEW YORK

It was time for a little bunny
to be on the move.
From here to there,
a bunny goes where a bunny must.

Bunny, Bunny going down the path,
Bunny, Bunny, aren't you turning back?

Where are you going, Little Bunny?

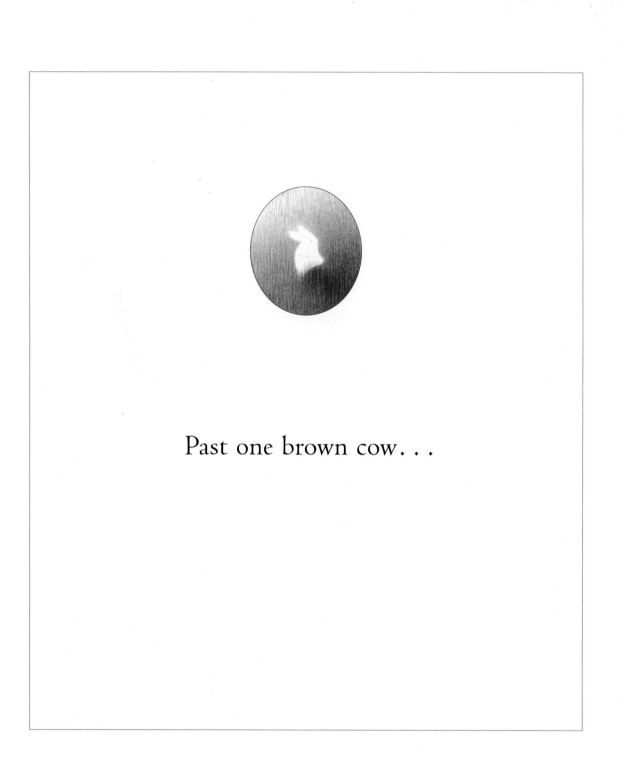

Past one brown cow. . .

past five fat sheep. . .

this bunny would not stop.

Over train tracks. . .

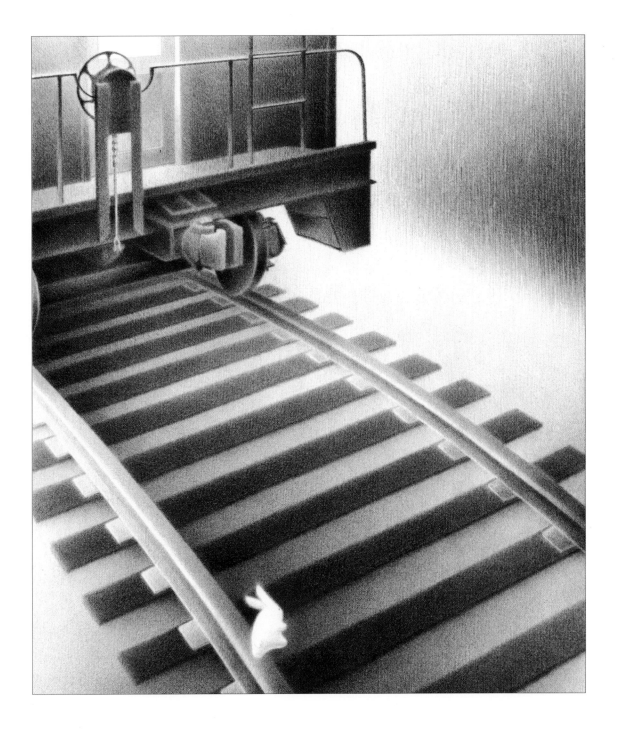

through a fence.

This bunny could not stop.
This bunny had a place to go.

Bunny, Bunny, the sky is turning black.
Bunny, Bunny, aren't you going back?

Won't you stop to sleep, Little Bunny?

"Hello, Little Bunny, hello!"

A voice wakes the sleeping bunny.

"Do you need a place to stay?
Do you need a home?"

"No thank you, not today!"

This bunny would not
be someone's pet.
This bunny would not stay.

Through the trees. . .

across an open field.

This bunny would not look back.
This bunny had come a long way.

Bunny, Bunny going up the hill,
Bunny, Bunny, can you not sit still?
Where are you going, Little Bunny?

"Here, I'm going here.

You see, I have a home."

And this bunny did have a home.
This bunny did have a place to stay.